Double
Trouble

WITHDRAWN

Other books in the
RSPCA ANIMAL TALES series

*The Million Paws Puppy*
*Ruby's Misadventure*
*An Unexpected Arrival*

# Double Trouble

## Helen Kelly

RANDOM HOUSE AUSTRALIA

A Random House book
Published by Random House Australia Pty Ltd
Level 3, 100 Pacific Highway, North Sydney NSW 2060
www.randomhouse.com.au

First published by Random House Australia in 2012

Addresses for companies within the Random House Group can be
found at www.randomhouse.com.au/offices

National Library of Australia
Cataloguing-in-Publication Entry

Author: Kelly, Helen
Title: Double Trouble / Helen Kelly
ISBN: 978 1 74275 330 0 (pbk)
Series: Animal tales; 3
Target Audience: For primary school age
Subjects: Animals – Juvenile fiction
         Dogs – Juvenile fiction
Dewey Number: A823.4

Cover photograph © Jerry Young/Getty Images
Internal photographs: image of cat by iStockphoto; image of horse by
Shutterstock; image of dog by Patricia Doyle/Getty Images
Cover and internal design by Ingrid Kwong
Internal illustrations by Charlotte Whitby
Typeset by Midland Typesetters, Australia
Printed in Australia by Griffin Press, an Accredited ISO AS/NZS
14001:2004 Environmental Management System printer

Random House Australia uses papers that are naural, renewable
and recyclable products and made from wood grown in sustainable
forests. The logging and manufacturing processes are expected to
conform to the environmental regulations of the country of origin.

# Chapter One

'Hi, Margaret!' chirped Cassie Bannerman as she came through the door of the Abbotts Hill RSPCA clinic.

'Hello, Cassie, what can I do for you today?' said Margaret, the clinic's receptionist. She knew Cassie well, as she and her mum and dad lived just up the road where they ran the local delicatessen.

'I need to buy some of those little liver dog treats. Ripper just loves them and we've run out! I might take two bags just to be sure.'

As Margaret got the treats, the door of the consulting room opened and two tiny terriers came tearing through. They looked very relieved to be out of there and yapped loudly to let everyone know they had no intention of going back!

Following them came a worried-looking elderly lady who Cassie recognised from the dog park and an amused-looking vet.

Cassie bent down to comfort the dogs. 'I bet you've both been very brave.' The dogs agreed completely and wriggled onto their backs to give Cassie better access to their tummies.

'Hi, Cass,' said Dr Joe the vet. 'Have you met Tommy and Tallulah before?'

'I think I've seen you at the dog park once or twice, haven't I?' Cassie asked the lady.

'Oh yes,' said Daisy Jones, the terriers' owner. 'I knew that I recognised you from somewhere! And Tommy and Tallulah never forget a face.'

'Vaccination time?' enquired Cassie.

'Well, yes, dear,' said Daisy. 'They're glad it's all over for another year and so am I.'

'They're Australian Terriers, aren't they?' asked Cassie. 'You don't see very many of them around. They're just gorgeous!'

'They are! Sweet little bundles of fun,' said Daisy. 'I've had Tommy and Tallulah since they were puppies. They're twins, you know. They're six years old now and we've never been apart.'

Just then there was a loud crash as the door to the clinic flew open, making both Cassie and Daisy jump. Daisy tutted as the terriers fled for cover under the closest chair and looked up crossly as a delighted looking Old English Sheepdog flounced in, towing a sweaty, scruffy boy behind her on a lead.

'Hi, Florence,' said Cassie with a laugh. 'You certainly know how to make an entrance, don't you? Were you taking Ben for his walk?' she joked as Florence bounced over for a pat.

'Daisy, this is my son, Ben,' said Dr Joe, 'and our dog, Florence.'

'Hello,' said Ben politely.

'Hey, Dad, I've walked Florence. After I drop her home, can I go back to the park for an hour? Danny's there and I said I'd have a quick game of footy with him before dinner.' Ben was already inching towards the door and was halfway through it before his dad had a chance to reply.

'Okay, but be back here by six!' yelled Dr Joe to the disappearing boy.

Cassie smiled. Ben was in her class at school and they'd grown to be quite good friends since he'd moved to Abbotts Hill a few months ago.

'Anyway, Daisy,' said Cassie, trying to put the elderly lady at ease again, 'you were saying you, Tommy and Tallulah have never been apart?'

'That's right,' said Daisy, as she bent to put Tommy's and Tallulah's leads on. 'I guess that's why I'm so worried about next week.'

'Why?' asked Cassie. 'What's happening then?'

'Well, I've been having trouble with one of my eyes and I have to go to hospital for a little operation to put it right. It means staying in hospital for two days, and of course I can't bring Tommy and Tallulah with me. I really don't know what to do. My neighbour is away on holiday, otherwise I would've asked him, and there's really no-one else . . .'

'Dr Joe! You run a service that could help, don't you?' Without waiting for his reply, Cassie scurried round to the other side of the reception desk and came back waving a leaflet titled, 'Do You Need Help With Your Pet?' She handed it over to Daisy and stared expectantly at Dr Joe.

'Well, yes, Cassie's right. It's a service we offer for people in exactly your situation –' he started.

'Yes, it's especially for people who are going into hospital and have no one to look after their pets!' interrupted Cassie.

'We can care for the pets here in the clinic for a limited time, or more likely send them to a suitable foster home with one of our volunteers,' continued Dr Joe.

'It's not just for that, though,' Cassie went on. 'It can be for older people who can no longer walk their dogs, or groom them or who just need a bit of help. And it's not even just dogs! They can help with any type of pet. And it won't cost you a fortune, either.'

Dr Joe raised an eyebrow and considered himself lucky to have got a word in at all. Within a few minutes Tommy and Tallulah were booked in for a three-day stay and Daisy Jones, looking much happier, headed home.

'Gosh, what time is it?' asked Cassie suddenly. 'Mum will be wondering where I've got to. Better go. Bye, Dr Joe!'

Cassie was almost through the door when she remembered what she'd come for and turned back to find Margaret, standing patiently with two bags of liver treats.

# Chapter Two

'Hi, Dad!' yelled Ben as he came through the door of the clinic the following Tuesday. He'd only got back from school half an hour ago, but Florence was itching to have a run and so they were heading to the park.

The clinic was super-busy. There were six people in the waiting area, as well as two bunnies, one marmalade cat, a German Shepherd, a chocolate-coloured Labrador puppy and a cardboard box with something that clucked unhappily every now and then. Ben's dad was nowhere to be seen.

'Is Dad around, Margaret?' he asked the receptionist.

'Hi, Ben,' she said. 'We've had such a busy day and the veterinary nurse has just had to go home sick, so your dad's here on his own. There must be something going round because I've had two of the volunteers ring in sick, too!'

'I just wanted to ask him for some money for a –' started Ben, but Margaret was holding up a finger to stop him as the phone started ringing and she ran to answer it.

Ben shrugged and started heading for the door. It looked as though his dad was pretty busy.

But then the door opened and a lady walked in with two yappy little terriers who, judging by the sounds they were making, were not very happy to be there.

'Good afternoon,' said Ben. 'Margaret will be with you in a minute. Do you have an appointment?'

Ben recognised the cross lady who had been in last week at the same moment that Daisy Jones recognised the scruffy and really rather rude boy that she'd met briefly the last time she'd been here.

Dr Joe popped his head out of the consulting room and, having seen Daisy, came over.

'Afternoon, Mrs Jones; now, there's been a bit of a change of plan. The volunteer who was going to take Tommy and Tallulah has actually called in sick and Margaret is trying to find a replacement for you. There seems to be a bit of a bug going round, and I know it's such short notice too. Normally I could keep them here, but you can see how busy we are; the clinic's full!'

'Oh dear,' said Daisy. 'So will you still be able to take them?'

'Well, I know that Cassie Bannerman is really good with animals, especially dogs. Her parents are registered carers for the RSPCA and they often help us out. We could see if they are able to mind them?' Dr Joe was quite pleased with this suggestion.

'Cassie?' said Ben. He was more than a bit miffed. Yes, Cassie was good with dogs, but so was he! He could mind these two terriers every bit as well as her! Better, even!

Daisy's face brightened. 'Oh yes, Cassie's a delightful girl, isn't she? Such a natural with dogs. So caring and polite.

'But we could mind them, Dad!' said Ben. 'Don't forget you're a registered carer too! And who better to mind them than a vet? The clinic might be full, but we have plenty of room at our house. Don't we, Dad?'

Both Daisy and Dr Joe looked at Ben as though they'd forgotten he was there.

'Could you, Dr Joe?' said Daisy. She seemed very hopeful indeed.

'I'd help too, Mrs Jones,' said Ben, warming to the idea the more he thought about it. 'I could do all the walking and the feeding after school and they could be here with Dad during the day.'

'Well . . .' said Daisy, looking at Dr Joe who was regarding his son thoughtfully.

Ben made one last attempt. 'Besides, Cassie is really busy at the moment. She's been training really hard for next week's cross-country race. It's taking every spare minute she has. She really wants to win her age group this year. And you know she lives close by if I need any help with them . . .'

Dr Joe shrugged at Daisy. 'Well, between the two of us it seems we're up for the job, Mrs Jones. What do you think?'

'It's only for three days and they're little angels, really,' said Daisy. 'So easy-going. And with Ben's help, of course . . .' Here she trailed off, appearing a little doubtful.

All three humans automatically looked down at the two angelic dogs sitting patiently. What could possibly go wrong?

# Chapter Three

Later, with Daisy Jones packed off to the hospital and his dad back at work, Ben was ready for the world. Formal introductions had been made and Florence, Tommy and Tallulah were getting on like old friends.

'Margaret, could you let Dad know I've headed off to the park with the dogs? I'll meet him back home later.'

'No problem, Ben. You're sure you'll be okay with all three at once?' asked Margaret, concerned.

'We'll be fine, won't we, T's?' said Ben confidently. Seriously, why was everyone worried? He was great with dogs! And anyway, Mrs Jones had said her dogs were angels.

Passing the deli, Ben saw Cassie inside and couldn't resist showing off his new dogs.

'Hey, Cassie!' he called out, 'we're heading to the dog park. Want to come?'

Cassie caught sight of the terriers and came out with a big smile on her face.

'Tommy and Tallulah! Hi, guys!' The terriers remembered Cassie and demanded lots of pats and tickles. 'Are you taking all three dogs?' asked Cassie.

'Yeah, I'm just helping Dad out. Mrs Jones was happy for me to mind them.' Ben sounded so proud of himself that Cassie had to smile.

'That'll keep you busy,' she said.

'Nothing I can't handle,' said Ben airily. 'So, are you coming?'

'Yes, I was just going to grab something to eat and then go over. Fancy a milkshake?'

'Mmm . . . that would depend on the flavour of the day,' said Ben, who had never yet been known to turn down the offer of a milkshake.

Cassie pondered. 'How about Sam's Surprise? Mum's speciality!' Without waiting for an answer, Cassie ran inside and ordered two.

'They're just too cute!' gushed Cassie as she went back out and took a seat at one of the tables. 'You're going to have so much fun staying with Ben, yes you are!' she told the little dogs as they clamoured for her attention.

'They're pretty friendly,' said Ben. 'They love Florence and they seem really well-behaved.'

'Hi, Ben, here we go!' said Cassie's mum, Sam, as she put the tray down. 'Two of my surprises for two of my best customers!' She smiled before going back into the shop.

'Hi, Ripper,' said Cassie as her dog bounced out to join them. 'Have you come to meet Ben's new pups?'

Ripper was the friendliest dog in the world, but to look at him you wouldn't know it. And the T's didn't know it. They didn't like the look of this big dog at all, and when Ripper smiled at them, the terriers were not impressed. The dogs were transformed into frantic, flying furballs. The high-pitched energetic yapping even raised a bewildered Florence to her feet. Pulling their leads out of Ben's hand, the terriers threw themselves at Ripper.

It could be considered lucky that the table was between Ripper and the terriers. Ripper was able to retreat quickly back to the safety of the shop. But the table? Not so lucky. The milkshakes flew into the air and the table crashed loudly onto its side.

The chairs flew backwards with an echoing BANG! BANG! as Ben and Cassie leapt to their feet just in time to grab one small milkshake-soaked dog each.

# Chapter Four

Ben turned to Cassie. Her face looked as horrified as he imagined his own did.

'Ahem!'

They both turned at the same time to see Mrs Bannerman standing in the door of the shop. Ben had never seen Cassie's mum angry, but he suspected it looked something like this.

'Sorry, Sam!' stammered Ben. 'Well, that certainly was a surprise, wasn't it?'

Cassie and Sam looked blankly at him.

'You know, Sam's "surprise", the flavour of the day?' he said, wishing he hadn't.

Cassie groaned at such a lame attempt at humour and handed Tommy, or Tallulah, she wasn't sure which, back to Ben.

'How about I clean up here and meet you at the park in a bit?' said Cassie. 'It might be better if we introduce Ripper on slightly more neutral ground.'

'Sure,' agreed Ben, relieved to be getting off so lightly.

'Sorry, Mum, I should have realised that such small dogs might find Ripper scary. They just seemed so friendly with Florence that I thought it would be okay,' Cassie said as she and Sam tackled the mess with a bucket of soapy water.

'It's okay, Cass, you should have seen your faces when I came out! It was almost worth it!' Sam had recovered her usual good humour. 'It's just that I seem to have spent the whole day cleaning! I was out in the garden early this morning and something had got into the compost heap and scattered the whole thing from one end of the garden to the other. It's as though someone had a huge food fight! It took me ages to clean it all up.'

'That's weird,' said Cassie, wiping down the last chair. 'There. As good as new!'

'Thanks, Cass,' said her mum. 'Now go and catch up with Ben and make sure he doesn't have any more "surprises" with those dogs!'

'I'll get Ripper and do a few training laps of the oval first. Only two more days before the cross-country race. See you later!'

At the dog park Ben soon regained his usual confidence and did a quick walk round the park with the T's on the lead, just to get them used to being there.

'You'll be fine here, won't you, Tommy? And you too, Tallulah! I bet you come here all the time. Let's get those leads off and you can have a proper run.'

The dogs loved being free of the leads and had a bit of a one-sided rumble with Florence while keeping pace with Ben.

Ben felt good. If only Margaret or his dad or Daisy Jones could see him now! Walking along with the three impeccably behaved dogs trailing behind him like little ducklings. At least Cassie would be here soon and see how capable and in control he was. He took a quick glance towards the gate, but there was still no sign of her.

All of a sudden, '*YAP! YAP! YAP!*' It was so high-pitched and so familiar that

Ben couldn't believe it wasn't Tommy or Tallulah. He looked down and there they were, all perky-eared, listening. Phew, the yapping had come from further away.

But Ben had *phew*-ed too early. The terriers bolted like a pair of mini-greyhounds out of the gate, yapping some more as they went. Florence wasn't going to miss out on mayhem! She raced off in pursuit.

Ben attempted to stroll casually after them but the yapping was so high-pitched! And there was so much of it! Ben was sure that every dog owner there was now watching the comical progress across the park – two tiny, excitable dogs and his great big adorable Flo. In a desperate bid to stop the procession, he abandoned all attempts at remaining cool and sprinted after them.

# Chapter Five

Just as Ben became convinced that Tommy and Tallulah were heading for the gate and that he'd never see them again, they stopped. Unfortunately their yapping didn't. In fact the sounds got even louder and then Ben realised that there were actually three Australian terriers yapping happily away at top volume. Tommy and Tallulah had met a friend.

'Hello, Tommy and Tal!' enthused a jolly woman, trying to cuddle each of them in turn. 'Monty was hoping you'd be here! Go on, have fun and play!' she said.

'Hi,' panted Ben, finally catching up to the group. 'Is everything okay?'

'Little Monty and the twins love to get together for a play. I didn't think we'd see them at all while Daisy is in the hospital. So this is a lovely surprise, isn't it, Monty? I see you have a new friend, Tommy and Tal! And a big one at that,' she said as she carefully patted a panting Florence on her head. Monty looked up at Flo, but thought it sensible to keep his distance.

The dogs certainly did seem happy. They tore around chasing each other for ages, never flagging or taking a rest and always accompanied by the high-pitched chorus of yaps. As the dogs played, Ben and Monty's owner walked around the park while Florence took it in turns sticking close to Ben and attempting to join in with the high-energy entertainment provided by the T's.

'Oh, Australian Terriers are just gorgeous, aren't they?' remarked the cheerful woman.

Ben nodded his agreement.

'So loyal and friendly,' she continued.

'You don't find them quite, um . . . yappy?' asked Ben.

'Yappy? No, no, they just love to talk, that's all. So sociable.' The woman was clearly a big fan of the Aussie Terrier and she talked on and on about the subject until the dogs had quite exhausted themselves. Ben was feeling pretty tired, too.

'Ah well, time to go!' declared the jolly woman at last. 'This is my gate here. So nice to meet you. It's wonderful what you're doing for Daisy. Keep up the good work! Come on, Monty!'

In one smooth movement she had leashed the unruly little dog and swept him off towards the car park.

Ben could just see Cassie coming in the gate at the far end, so he directed his tired little dog posse in her direction.

'Hi,' said Cassie as she reached him. 'How's it going?'

'Well, I think we've recovered from our shaky start, haven't we, Florence?' said Ben. 'Your mum's face, though. She seemed really mad,' he said, attempting a look of concern before giving up and snorting with laughter.

Cassie couldn't help but join in. She stopped short after glancing over at the terriers.

'Ben, aren't Tommy's and Tallulah's tags pink and blue?' she asked.

'Yeah, I think so,' said Ben, looking down at the dogs.

The red name tag on one of the dogs seemed to glow!

Cassie read the red tag. 'So if this is Monty, where's Tommy?' she asked.

Ben was utterly bewildered. He looked at the gate on the far side of the park and beyond that he could see Monty's owner unlocking her car and popping a dog she thought was hers inside!

# Chapter Six

'Oh my goodness!' declared Monty's owner between chuckles.

Ben had managed to catch her and explain the mix-up before she took off with Tommy.

'You know, I thought Monty seemed a bit different. A little less thrilled about jumping into my car,' she carried on. 'Wait until I tell Daisy all about this! She'll laugh and laugh!'

Off went the jolly woman, with Monty none the worse for wear. Ben's nerves were a little frayed. He turned to Tallulah. 'You could have let me know I'd taken the wrong dog, Tallulah.'

Tallulah panted back at him happily, not willing to take responsibility for anything.

Ben avoided making eye contact with Cassie as he fixed up both terriers' leads. Tommy and Tallulah now looked ready for a good lie-down. Even Florence seemed weary.

'I think we'll head home,' said Ben dolefully.

'I doubt they've ever had that much exercise in a single afternoon.' Cassie smiled as they all turned towards home.

'So funny,' replied Ben moodily.

'Well, look on the bright side, it's all good training for the cross-country race. I haven't seen you training. You are taking part, aren't you?' she asked Ben.

'An afternoon of running round and round the park instead of sitting in class doing maths? You bet I'm running. I'm pretty fast too, so you better watch out.'

Cassie grinned to herself. It never took Ben long to get back on form.

By the time Ben and his dad sat down to their shepherd's pie dinner, the terriers had been bathed and dried and looked a picture of cute fluffiness. Ben had washed them both when he got home so that his dad wouldn't notice that they smelled of milkshake. Which meant that it would be completely unnecessary to go into detail of any of the afternoon's mishaps.

'They look exhausted, Ben! You certainly gave them a good run this evening,' said Dr Joe.

Ben glanced over to the crate that the T's were sharing in the corner of the kitchen. Their little eyes were closing and they seemed perfectly contented.

'Yeah, they met a friend at the park and ran and ran for ages. They haven't touched their food, though. Do you think they're missing Daisy?' asked Ben.

'Bound to be,' said Dr Joe. 'Daisy says they've never been apart. If we leave the crate open, they'll be able to get the food if they want it in the night. Don't worry, they'll eat when they're hungry enough.'

'You know best. You're the vet,' said Ben.

'This is true,' replied Dr Joe. 'Anyway, let's get all this tidied up. Mum's on the late shift, so she won't be back for hours. Have you got any homework to do?' he asked as he started clearing away the dinner plates.

'Just finishing up the rainforests project. It's due tomorrow,' said Ben.

'And how's it looking?' asked Joe.

'See for yourself,' said Ben and started piling his homework out onto the table. 'I've focused on tropical animals. I'm pretty pleased with it. Just got to finish colouring in the last of the pictures.'

'Impressive,' said Joe. 'Your drawings are great! Looks like you spent ages on it. Well done!'

'Thanks, Dad!' Ben grinned.

A couple of hours later, with the project finally finished to his satisfaction, Ben yawned, grabbed a glass of milk for himself and said goodnight to Tommy and Tallulah. They were very different dogs to the pair that had caused so much havoc this afternoon. They'd still not eaten anything. Ben hoped they weren't actually sick rather than just homesick. What would he say to Daisy Jones if something happened to her beloved T's while they were in his care?

He went up to bed, leaving his bedroom door open so he could hear them if they needed him in the night.

# Chapter Seven

'Ben, wake up! Come on, it's already eight o'clock! You'll be late for school!' yelled Ben's mum, Veronica.

Ben was bleary-eyed as he came down the stairs. Florence was snoring softly from her basket underneath the kitchen table. Tommy and Tallulah looked peaceful as they slept soundly, curled up together in their crate. Dr Joe and Dr Veronica Stoppard were hunched over their coffee and muesli at the kitchen table, seemingly grumpy.

'Sleep well?' Ben's mum asked as he took his seat at the table.

'No, not really,' replied Ben.

'Neither did we. The yapping gets really shrill after a while, doesn't it?' said Veronica, gently massaging her temples.

The terriers had yapped and whined all night long. Ben and his dad had been up and down the stairs, settling them every half hour throughout the night. It must have been after 4 am that his mum had thought of filling a hot water bottle and putting it in with the terriers. She'd put the radio on and turned the volume low so they wouldn't get lonely, and only then had the humans in the Stoppard household been able to finally get some rest.

Ben's dad yawned. 'They'll be fine tonight, you'll see. They were just a bit homesick.'

Ben and his mum looked at each other, eyebrows raised, before carrying on with their breakfast.

'You better feed them here, Ben, then I'll take them into the clinic this morning,' said Dr Joe.

'Okay, thanks, Dad.' Ben wolfed down his brekkie and then went for the kibble.

Tommy and Tallulah woke up and started the day with a whole body shake that nearly wriggled them right off their feet.

'You really are very cute!' Veronica said, losing the frown and giving Tommy a little tummy rub. 'But what have you been rolling in?'

'Huh?' asked Ben a little guiltily, wondering if some of yesterday's milkshake was still there.

'There are little bits of goo all over his tummy and tail –' Veronica had picked up the dog and was removing the sticky little bits from Tommy's coat and piling them on the table '– and back. Oh, and his head. What are they?'

'That's weird!' said Dr Joe as he picked up Tallulah. 'She's covered in them, too! What is it? It's almost like chewed-up bits of paper; they're all different colours.'

Ben was watching the pile of colourful sticky mush growing on the table as his parents patiently picked the dogs clean. Definitely not milkshake. But he couldn't help feeling that the colours looked vaguely familiar. He frowned. 'They're in the crate as well.'

Ben grabbed the red fleecy blanket that lined the crate and gave it a shake. Small gooey pellets went everywhere! There were hundreds of them and there were still plenty stuck to the blanket too.

'Oh no,' cried Ben, realisation dawning. 'Somebody tell me this isn't really happening!

There, in the bottom of the crate, the only thing left apart from the goo, lay the remains of Ben's rainforest project.

There were no straight edges left, just a lumpy soggy mess held together with a bulldog clip.

Veronica picked it up and managed to separate the pages. You could still see parts of the beautiful toucans and chameleons that Ben had lovingly drawn, but there was not much she could say that would make Ben feel better. 'I'll get my hairdryer, Ben, we'll have it dried out it no time. Just hand in what you have and explain what happened to Mrs Smith.'

Ben was fuming. 'Great! I'll say the dogs ate my homework and she'll think it's just a bad excuse. But I really did the work.'

Dr Joe stifled a chuckle.

Ben turned on his dad. 'Dad, it's not funny!'

'Sorry, son, I know. I was recalling how often I tried that old dog-eared excuse out on my teacher when I was at school.'

'Did it ever work?' asked Ben, vaguely amused despite the situation.

'Never,' replied Dr Joe with a wry grin.

Ben looked at the T's, who were watching him with big baleful eyes. They really did look sorry, didn't they? This dog-sitting business was much more hard work than he'd ever imagined. 'Two more days. Just two more days,' he repeated to himself.

Florence let out another snore from underneath the table, oblivious to all the drama.

# Chapter Eight

After school Ben picked Florence up from the house and headed over to the clinic with a heavy heart. He was feeling tired and grumpy. His mum had been right – Mrs Smith had understood and had even found it quite funny. But that didn't help with the fact that she'd left the whole pile of projects on her desk all day. And they all looked terrific, except for his chewed-up mess.

'Hi, Ben!' said Margaret. 'Tommy and Tallulah have been waiting for you!' She turned towards the terriers. 'You're ready for a run, aren't you?'

They certainly were. The T's had slept all day and now they were full of energy and ready to play.

'Right,' declared Ben. 'We are staying at the park until these two are completely exhausted! Okay, Flo?' Florence agreed and off they went.

Determined to be more in control today, Ben tiptoed past the Bannermans' deli, hoping to avoid a repeat of yesterday's performance. Ripper was nowhere to be seen, but the two T's started their frantic pulling and yapping anyway! The volume went up and up. Ben walked faster and faster, trying not to draw attention to himself. After he'd passed the shop, he broke into a run, just to be on the safe side. What was wrong with these dogs?! Once they were a good distance from the deli, they quietened down again.

'Hi, Ben!' yelled Cassie a minute later as Ben turned a corner and entered the dog park.

'Hi,' said Ben, trying to ignore Florence's over-excitement at seeing Ripper. 'Still training for the cross country?'

'Yep, nearly done,' she panted. 'Two more laps and then I'll join you.'

Cassie sprinted off around the outside of the dog park, and with Ripper on the lead looking every bit as determined as she did. Ben had to admit she was pretty fast. He wondered if he'd left it too late to start some training himself. The race was tomorrow, so he probably had. Oh well! Ben figured that as long as he didn't finish last he wasn't too bothered.

He carried on into the park before realising that the terriers hadn't yapped at Ripper. They'd let him run on by beside Cassie without so much as a whimper. He didn't understand what made these dogs tick at all!

After tiring the canines out, Cassie and Ben were walking home and chatting about their day. But as they came close to Cassie's place, the two terriers erupted into frenzied barking again!

'I don't believe it!' said Cassie. 'It's not Ripper they're barking at – it's the shop itself. How strange!'

Samantha Bannerman had heard them coming and had made a speedy appearance at the door of the shop.

'Hi, kids,' said Sam. 'And hello to you too, Double Trouble,' she said as she bent down to calm the frantic T's. 'How are they settling in, Ben? No problems?'

'We're getting on fine now.' Ben was still embarrassed about the day before and changed the subject quickly.

'Cassie was telling me about your mysterious ransacker. Have you had any luck catching the culprit?' he asked.

'No, and it happened again last night! That's the second night running. It can't just be a coincidence, can it?' said Sam with a wicked grin.

'What can't?' said Ben.

'Well, my compost heap is mysteriously scattered about at the same time those two very yappy and excitable dogs start taking an interest in my shop!'

'But, Mrs B, the T's couldn't have done it!' stammered Ben. 'They've not been out of my sight all evening! And there are two more witnesses at my house who will tell you that they never left the house last night!' Ben yawned at the very thought of the night before and hoped that Sam wouldn't actually question his parents.

But Sam was joking and Cassie grinned. *Very funny*, he thought. Clearly a strange sense of humour ran in the family.

'Well, I'll be listening out for signs of trouble tonight,' said Sam as she went back inside.

# Chapter Nine

'I sometimes think there is nothing in the world as amazing as a good night's sleep!' said Ben's mum the next morning as she came down the stairs. 'Don't you just feel ready for the day?' she asked Ben.

'Yes, Mum,' agreed Ben without taking his eyes off the cereal box he was reading.

Ben wasn't a morning person but, to be honest, he felt pretty good too. The T's had slept through the night and were at this moment rumbling with Florence in the garden after eating a hearty breakfast. Nothing had been damaged, no-one had been yapped at and there had been no sudden and unexplained mood swings. Things were definitely getting better.

'Dad had to go in early this morning,' explained Veronica, 'so do you have time to drop the T's off at the vet on your way to school?'

'Yep, plenty of time today,' said Ben and he grabbed his bag and the terriers' leads.

'I'll see you at the cross-country race later!' yelled his mum as he headed out the door. 'Good luck!'

DOG

The frantic yapping started when they were two shops away from the deli. Even though Ben had expected the reaction, he could still feel himself panicking and wanting to break into a run. They were so noisy! Cassie had heard the chaos from inside the shop and popped her head out the door.

'You're early today! Heading to school?'

Ben nodded.

'Hang on a minute, I'll grab my school-bag and come with you,' shouted Cassie over the din. As she went back inside, the door to the deli swung open and the terriers flew through.

Ben chased after them a moment later, following the yapping noise through the shop to the other side, where he came face-to-face with a startled and unhappy-looking Mrs B. *Oops.* Gladiator the cat sauntered out from under the table with a half-smile on her face. Oh yes, those yappy terriers were in serious trouble now.

# Chapter Ten

The terriers sidestepped Mrs Bannerman and tore through the shop and into the back area, where Mr Bannerman was having a relaxing morning coffee before the start of his working day. Ben was a few steps behind the terriers, and offered Cassie's dad an apologetic shrug before following the dogs out the open kitchen door and into the back garden.

By the time Mr and Mrs Bannerman and Cassie also arrived in the garden, a strange silence filled the air. The T's were nowhere to be seen, but the contents of the compost heap were being flung far and wide. Food, vegetable peelings, soil, coffee grounds and grass clippings were being scattered the length and breadth of the garden.

Ben wasn't sure how he was even going to *start* apologising for this mess. The Bannermans were speechless.

'Tommy, Tallulah, COME HERE!' said Ben in his sternest voice.

The terriers failed to appear from the mess but something else did. One ... two little furry bodies came flying out of the mess and made for the closest tree before disappearing at an amazing speed off into the lower branches.

Everyone was speechless.

'Mum, look! Did you see? Possums!' cried Cassie.

'Tommy! Tallulah! Come!' repeated Ben firmly.

Out of the debris came two creatures that walked and behaved like Australian Terriers. They sat, looking expectantly up at Ben, but were so coated with soil and sticky stuff, coffee and flour, they were hard to recognise. Yet underneath all the grime, their angelic little faces looked so perfectly happy and friendly that it was hard not to smile. Ben struggled to stay serious. He was trying to come up with something to say, when Cassie saved him.

'The T's have found our mysterious bandits! I knew they weren't being naughty!' She laughed.

Mrs B wasn't entirely sure this was true, but gave a weak smile. Gladiator yawned, raised her tail in the air and went back to her comfy spot under the table.

'I'm so sorry about the mess, Sam. I can come back after school and help you clean it up if you like?' said Ben.

'I think you've done enough already, Ben. Thanks, though,' replied Sam.

'Two tiny heroes! That's what you are!' cooed Cassie at the messy little T's.

'Ben!' called out Dr Joe as Ben and Cassie walked into the clinic twenty minutes later. 'Good news! Daisy's operation has gone so well that she's been discharged this morning. She's really missed the T's and plans to pick them up around lunchtime.'

Ben and Cassie looked down at the Tommy and Tallulah, unsure of quite what to say.

'Arrgh!' Dr Joe stepped back in fright when he caught sight of the terriers still covered in compost and definitely not smelling their best. 'But they were looking so clean and fluffy this morning when I left home . . .'

Margaret was holding her nose. 'What do they smell of? I can't put my finger on it, but it's not particularly good.'

'Let's just say the T's have proved them-selves heroes this morning!' declared Ben. 'And for the longer version of the story, you may have to wait until this afternoon. We don't want to be late for school!'

'Do you think we have time to give the T's a bit of a bath?' asked Cassie. 'I'd hate Daisy to see them like this.'

'Don't worry, Cassie, they will be their own cute, fluffy selves within the hour, I'll make sure of it,' Margaret assured her. 'Now off to school!'

# Chapter Eleven

Abbotts Hill Park looked very different after lunch. The whole of Abbotts Hill Public School was there in their sporting colours. Clusters of kids in blue, green, red and yellow filled every available space along the track to cheer on their fellow students.

Cassie and Ben stood at the starting line for the last race of the day – years five and six.

The principal was on the loudspeaker, issuing final instructions. 'So twice around the entire park and then a further two laps round the outside of the dog oval before finishing on the far side by the cricket pavilion,' he said. 'There are parent helpers at every turn should you need assistance but, if in doubt, just follow the flags!'

Cassie was going over and over it in her head. She had run the course so often in the past few weeks that she felt she could probably do it in her sleep, though she was still worried about missing a bit somewhere along the line.

'Good luck, everybody. On your marks, get set and . . . GO!'

They were off. Cassie got into a good position right at the start and didn't look back. She didn't even turn her head to see where everyone else was, she just wanted to reach the end. Cassie had come fifth in the cross country every single year that she'd taken part. This year she was determined to receive a ribbon at assembly!

By the second lap of the dog park Cassie was fairly sure she was well ahead. There was a chance she might actually win! But suddenly she could hear someone calling her name, followed by laughter. What was going on? Her concentration was slipping as she looked around and noticed the surrounding crowd was pointing and laughing; seemingly at her!

She turned her head to the right and noticed two small Aussie Terriers keeping pace with her on the inside of the fence. Tommy and Tallulah were sprinting away, doing their best to stay alongside Cassie. On her left a year-six girl was gaining on her.

With a final burst of energy, helped by the encouragement of her canine friends, Cassie sprinted towards the finish line to take . . . first place!

# Chapter Twelve

'That was the funniest thing, Cassie!' said Ben, cracking up all over again.

'Tommy and Tallulah helped me win,' remarked Cassie, smiling affectionately at the two dogs, who were happily panting away next to Daisy Jones.

The Bannermans, the Stoppards and Daisy were all enjoying a celebratory afternoon tea in the Bannermans' garden.

'Time for a toast!' said Veronica Stoppard, holding up her cappuccino. 'To Cassie, for coming first in the cross country! And to Ben, for coming fifth!'

Everyone cheered and clinked their coffees and milkshakes.

'Fifth is pretty good, considering the amount of training you *didn't* do,' said Cassie with a laugh.

'I know,' said Ben. 'I'll try harder next year and get myself a ribbon.'

'I'd like to propose a toast too,' said Alex Bannerman, Cassie's dad. 'To Tommy and Tallulah, for discovering our mysterious night-time visitors! If you will all observe the new composting arrangements in the Bannerman garden!' he declared with a flourish, while directing all eyes to the brand-new compost bin in the corner by the fence. 'It is all sealed in with a lid and will never again be home to any unwelcome and messy visitors.'

Cups were clinked again and everyone laughed and cheered. It was only Cassie's worried face that spoiled the moment.

'But, Dad, what about the possums? Where will they live now?' she asked.

'Aha!' declared Alex theatrically. 'Look up!'

Everyone at the table looked up. Among the highest branches of the tree a wooden box was just visible.

'A possum nesting-box! Dad, you think of everything!' praised Cassie, throwing her arms around her dad's neck.

'A possum hotel, Cass. And it's far enough off the ground that they'll have to do their own tidying up!' said Alex, and everyone laughed.

'Do we have time for one final toast?' asked Daisy Jones. 'To Dr Joe, who has taken such wonderful care of my twins these past few days. I don't think I've ever seen them so contented! Look at their beautiful shiny coats!'

'I'm not sure I can toast to that, Daisy,' said Dr Joe before anyone could cheer. 'I'd be taking credit where it's not really due. If the T's are happy and contented, it's because Ben has done a really wonderful job of taking care of them and I think they've all enjoyed every minute.'

Ben, knowing he was surrounded by the people who had witnessed his many failings as a dog carer over the past two days, decided it was best to smile and say nothing.

'You know, if I ever had to go into hospital again I think I'd have to ask you to take care of them! They clearly adore you!' continued Daisy. 'So, here's to Ben!'

Ben and Cassie clinked their milkshake glasses together.

'To Tommy and Tallulah!' they cheered.

RSPCA

## ABOUT THE RSPCA

The RSPCA is the country's best known and most respected animal welfare organisation. The first RSPCA in Australia was formed in Victoria in 1871, and the organisation is now represented by RSPCAs in every state and territory.

The RSPCA's mission is to prevent cruelty to animals by actively promoting their care and protection. It is a not-for-profit charity that is firmly based in the Australian community, relying upon the support of individuals, businesses and organisations to survive and continue its vital work.

Every year, RSPCA shelters throughout Australia accept over 150,000 sick, injured or abandoned animals from the community. The RSPCA believes that every animal is entitled to the Five Freedoms:

# Fact File

- freedom from hunger and thirst (ready access to fresh water and a healthy, balanced diet)
- freedom from discomfort, including accommodation in an appropriate environment that has shelter and a comfortable resting area
- freedom from pain, injury or disease through prevention or rapid diagnosis and providing veterinary treatment when required

- freedom to express normal behaviour, including sufficient space, proper facilities and company of the animal's own kind

and

- freedom from fear and distress through conditions and treatment that avoid suffering.

# PETS OF OLDER PERSONS

*(taken from RSPCA NSW website)*

The Pets of Older Persons (POOPs) program assists socially isolated elderly people by offering assistance with their pets in times of crisis. The POOPs Program aims to keep pets and their elderly owners happy, healthy and together in their own homes for as long as possible.

POOPs was established by the Aged Care Assessment Team (ACAT) at St Joseph's Hospital Auburn in 2003 to temporarily care for the pets of elderly people who were admitted to hospital. The RSPCA became involved to provide assistance with veterinary care and emergency boarding.

POOPs is based in Sydney but assists clients throughout NSW whenever possible through RSPCA NSW Shelters and Branches.

# Fact File

### POOPs services:
• Temporary foster accommodation and/or emergency boarding of the pet should the owner require medical treatment, respite or other assistance
• Assistance with veterinary treatment at the RSPCA Sydney Vet Hospital
• Assistance with pet grooming
• Home visits to assist the elderly with basic pet care

### Who is eligible for POOPs?
POOPs is specifically designed to help people 65 years of age or older who are socially isolated and require assistance with care of their pets.

Palliative care patients of any age who are socially isolated may also access POOPs services.

As services differ in different states and territories, please check the RSPCA website to find out what services are offered in your area.
www.rspca.org.au

Please note that RSPCA foster carers are carefully selected and trained. Unlike this fictional representation, animals in foster are under adult care.

# RSPCA 🐾

# Animal

# AVAILABLE NOW

**COLLECT THEM ALL**

# COMING SEPTEMBER 2012

**THERE'S SO MUCH MORE AT RANDOMHOUSE.COM.AU/KIDS**